The Party Diaries

Top Secret Anniversary

written by
Mitali Banerjee Ruths

art by
Aaliya Jaleel

BRANCHES
SCHOLASTIC INC.

J
TRANS
RUT

To Ma and Baba, also known as Madhuri and Probir,
and to Jason Gillman and Jayeeta Ghosh —MBR

For Salman—AJ

Text copyright © 2023 by Mitali Banerjee Ruths
Art copyright © 2023 by Aaliya Jaleel

Library of Congress Cataloging-in-Publication Data

Names: Ruths, Mitali Banerjee, author. | Jaleel, Aaliya, illustrator.
Title: Top secret anniversary / written by Mitali Banerjee Ruths ; illustrated by Aaliya Jaleel.
Description: First edition. | New York : Branches/Scholastic, Inc., 2023. |
Series: The party diaries ; 3 | Audience: Ages 5–7. | Audience: Grades K–2. |
Summary: At her mother's request, Priya is planning a surprise anniversary party for her father, but she is finding it hard to keep it a secret from her inquisitive dad.
Identifiers: LCCN 2022034059 (print) | ISBN 9781338799903 (paperback) |
ISBN 9781338799910 (library binding)
Subjects: LCSH: East Indian Americans—Juvenile fiction. | Anniversaries—Juvenile fiction. |
Parties—Juvenile fiction. | Fathers and daughters—Juvenile fiction. | Secrecy—Juvenile fiction. |
CYAC: East Indian Americans—Fiction. | Anniversaries—Fiction. | Parties—Fiction. | Fathers and daughters—Fiction. | Secrets—Fiction. | LCGFT: Fiction. Classification: LCC PZ7.1.R9 To 2023 (print) |
DDC [Fic]—dc23
LC record available at https://lccn.loc.gov/2022034059

10 9 8 7 6 5 4 3 2 1   23 24 25 26 27

Printed in China   62
First edition, October 2023

Edited by Katie Carella
Book design by Maria Mercado

MIX
Paper from
responsible sources
FSC® C020056
www.fsc.org

11/23 - $7

TABLE OF CONTENTS

VIP LIST
(Very Important People)

Ma
(My mom, also known as Reeta)

Priya
(Me!)

Baba
(My dad, also known as Ashok)

Dida
(My grandmother is my mom's mom.)

Samir
(My little brother, also known as Sammy)

Mr. Williams
(Melissa's dad)

Vivek Uncle
(Layla Aunty's husband)

Layla Aunty
(My mom's best friend)

Dr. Williams
(Melissa's mom)

Melissa

Dola

My friends!

SECRET PLANS

Hello, world! It's Priya. Remember me?

I run my own party-planning business called Priya's Parties! Every party I plan raises money for an endangered animal!

So far, my business has helped quokkas and pangolins.

Let me tell you about running a business.

Writing plans in my party diary

Making DIY crafts
(Do-It-Yourself)

Crossing things off my to-do list

Being in charge
(I am a boss!)

Wondering if people will enjoy the party

Being okay with doing my best, even if it's not THE best

Learning how to stay calm when I need to get a lot done

Being in charge (It's hard work!)

Planning my next party will be a challenge. My mom hired me! See what she posted—

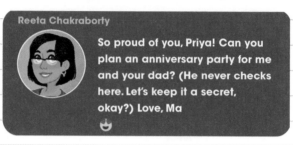

Reeta Chakraborty

So proud of you, Priya! Can you plan an anniversary party for me and your dad? (He never checks here. Let's keep it a secret, okay?) Love, Ma

So I'm planning a TOP SECRET party for next Saturday! That's the day my parents got married.

Reeta & Ashok's Wedding

I waited until Baba was NOT at home. Then I talked to Ma about the party.

Why is the party a secret?

I want to do something unexpected. A surprise before Baba and I go out to dinner!

I won't tell!

If I were Baba, I'd like to know that people were coming to my house! I'm not sure about this plan.

2

MY PARENTS

Sunday

Ma asked me to invite just a few guests.

PARTY PEOPLE

Dida & Sammy

Layla Aunty

Vivek Uncle

Melissa

Mr. Williams

Dr. Williams

Now I need party ideas. So I have to think about Ma and Baba . . .

They are mostly a good team.

But they sometimes argue about silly things.

They are interesting people together, and on their own.

MA

Ma makes up lyrics because she does not remember the words to ANY songs.

Ma likes making pickles.

cucumber pickles   mango pickles   lemon pickles   carrot pickles

BABA

Baba makes good homemade pizza. He also tells bad dad jokes.

Baba likes taking photos. He uses a camera that prints them out!

I thought a lot about my parents today, but I still have no idea what kind of party they would like.

HOW I'M FEELING

Grateful! This party will help an endangered animal.

Confused! What's the best way to celebrate Ma and Baba?

Nervous! Will Baba be surprised? Will everyone have fun at the party?

Yeeks! Where do I start?!

BRAINSTORM BUDDY

I need help brainstorming this party. So I went to Melissa's backyard after school.

I have no idea how my parents met. But I know who would know!

I'll ask Dida!

Yay! Then you can pick a party theme from how they met!

I raced home to talk to Dida. I couldn't find her, but I found Sammy outside the bathroom.

Dida is washing her hair. Then she'll read me ten books!

Dida will be busy for a while.

I took out my party diary.
Time to make a list!

ANNIVERSARY PARTY TO-DO LIST:

- Pick an endangered animal

- Choose a theme

- Make and deliver invitations

- Make DIY decorations

I can cross off one thing. My friend Dola
did a class presentation about Florida.
Manatees live there!
So I've been thinking
about manatees.

WHY MANATEES ARE SPECIAL

Manatees are the ocean's largest vegetarians! They eat sea plants.

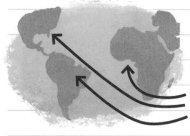

Manatees live around Florida, West Africa, and the Amazon River.

They are more related to elephants than to animals that live in water.

Manatees can weigh more than a grand piano! (Over 1,000 pounds!)

Suddenly, Baba popped into my room. So I hid my party diary FAST!

Hello, hi! Time for dinner.

Quick question—would you choose to have a third eye or a third ear?

Um, neither?

Baba asks lots of strange questions. At least he did not ask about my next party.

At dinner, Sammy ALMOST spilled the secret!

This Saturday is special! It's the day Ma and I got married!

We'll be going out to dinner.

And we'll have the party!

Ha-ha! It'll <u>feel</u> like a party! Because it's their anniversary!

Planning this surprise will be VERY tricky!

NEW SUITS

I am inventing an organized way to plan awesome parties! So I'm coming up with party-planning rules. Here's a new one.

Dig Deep Rule:

Learn about who the party is for.

17

After school, I finally got to talk with Dida.

Ma asked me to plan a secret anniversary party. Can you tell me how she met Baba?

Dida showed me old photos.

After college, your mom had to buy a suit to wear for job interviews.

Here is my parents' story . . .

Once upon a time, Ma went to the mall to find the perfect suit. She met Baba at a suit shop. He was looking for a suit, too.

That suit looks like it was made for you.

Thanks! I have a job interview. My name is Reeta, by the way.

Hello, hi! I'm Ashok! I'm also looking for a job. Well . . . Best of luck, Reeta!

A few weeks later, Ma and Baba saw each other at the mall again.

Reeta! Hello, hi!

Ashok, right? Guess what! I got the job!

Congratulations! I'm still looking.

Don't give up! Can I buy you a pretzel?

Ma and Baba ate pretzels in the food court. That was their first date.

Ma and Baba's story is romantic and NOT romantic.

ROMANTIC

Boy meets girl.

Girl buys boy a pretzel.

They get married!

NOT ROMANTIC

It's Ma and Baba.

Their first date was at the MALL.

They argue about toothpaste!

Dida showed me her wedding photo next. My grandfather died when I was little, so I don't know much about him.

Dadu

Priya, your parents were a love match. But Dadu and I had an arranged marriage. Our parents set up our first meeting.

Was that awkward?

I would not like a SURPRISE first date.

We were shy at first. But he became my best friend.

Thanks for sharing these stories, Dida.

Now I need to choose a party theme.

I could make a
pretend suit shop
with suits from Ma
and Baba's closet!

And I could bake
pretzels, like they had
on their first date!

Ooh! I'll make
cardboard hearts,
too! An anniversary
is all about love!

I can't wait to tell Melissa my ideas!

INVITATIONS

Melissa is a trustworthy friend. I can count on her to tell me the truth (in a nice way).

Melissa and I made collage invitations. We found magazines and cut out pictures of people wearing suits. Then we drew hearts.

Please wear your best suit to Reeta and Ashok's
TOP SECRET ANNIVERSARY PARTY!
Snacks will be served.

Chakraborty House
Saturday
5–7 p.m.

P.S. This party is hosted by Priya's Parties to help manatees.

Suddenly, Baba showed up!

Melissa and I lay on the invitations. I felt
a glue stick poking my back. My heart was
pounding!

Melissa can say my last name PERFECTLY
(like *chuck-ruh-burr-tee*). Real friends know
how to say your name the way you want
people to say it.

After Baba left, Melissa and I laughed. We had magazine scraps stuck to our clothes.

First, we gave Melissa's dad an invitation.

I wrote down the jokes.

Next, we biked
to Layla Aunty and
Vivek Uncle's house.

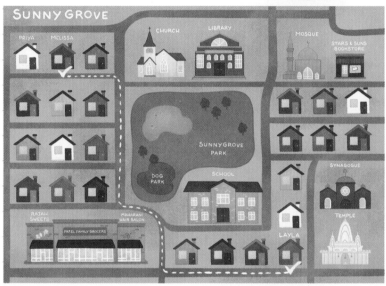

Then we stopped to
see the ducks.

I had one invitation
left—for Sammy and Dida.

The party plan is coming together!

I updated my to-do list. That means I added things . . .

ANNIVERSARY PARTY TO-DO LIST:

- ~~Pick an endangered animal~~
- ~~Choose a theme~~
- ~~Make and deliver invitations~~
- Make DIY decorations
- Bake PRETZELS!
- Set up the suit shop!

Will I get everything done? Tomorrow is DIY Decorations Day!

DIY DECORATIONS DAY

Thursday

Today at lunch, I told Dola her Florida project inspired me to help manatees. She was excited!

Go, Priya's Parties! I love it!

I feel super happy I started my business! But I have lots to do before my party can help manatees!

On our walk back to class, Melissa listened to my worries.

I still need to make decorations, bake pretzels, find my parents' suits for the suit shop . . .

Don't worry, Priya! This party will be awesome! You're a pro!

Melissa's dad picked me and Melissa up after school.

I have a party decoration idea!
Your dad loves taking photos.
What if we DIY a giant photo frame?!

Ooh! YES!

I feel lucky to have Melissa helping me. I even thought of a new rule!

Be Open Rule:

Hear ideas from
your team!

We did our DIY projects in Melissa's backyard. First, we painted big cardboard hearts.

TAILOR-made
for love

CUT from the
same CLOTH

The perfect FIT!

Then we made a big photo frame.

Melissa will keep the decorations at her house until the party.

Thanks, Melissa! Bye, Harry!

When I got to my room, I flopped on my bed. I was tired. But I still have more to do! And the party is the day after tomorrow! YEEKS!

SUIT SPY

Friday

Today is Fun, Fun Friday. It's a family fun night!
We make pizza and watch movies together.

To get ANY party prep done, I needed Sammy's help! I told him he had an important job. I hope he can do it.

Ma and Baba can't come in their room. If they leave the kitchen, say our secret signal.

Okay!

I ran into my parents' closet to look for suits and photos of Ma and Baba.

I have to be super sneaky. I don't want them to know I borrowed anything.

It is very stressful to sneak around your own house! I checked the hallway. Then I scurried out with my arms full.

I was almost to my room when I tripped and landed with a THUD.

I sprang up and hid everything behind my pillows.

Just then, Sammy ran in, yelling our secret signal.

Quack! Quack!

I had told Sammy to quack if our parents were coming. Maybe that wasn't my best idea.

I heard a thump! Is everything okay?

Yup! Just top secret party stuff.

This party is a surprise for Baba. But I want to surprise Ma, too.

We ate pizza and watched a movie. But my mind was on tomorrow's party.

SETTING UP SHOP

Saturday Morning

Baba made heart-shaped waffles for breakfast.

Happy anniversary!

I gave Ma a secret look—I needed her and Baba to leave the house!

We have so many errands today, Ashok.

What errands? It's our anniversary! We should relax at home.

You could relax at the art museum!

Wonderful idea!

After breakfast, I found Ma and Baba in the bathroom.

FINALLY, my parents were ready to leave. Ma winked at me.

It was pretzel time at last! Dida, Sammy, and I jumped into action. We rolled dough into long snakes. Then we twisted the snakes into pretzels.

All of mine turned out wonky.

BEST PRETZELS

Dida's   Sammy's   Mine

Pretzel making took longer than I thought. I am running out of time! YEEKS!

Melissa texted me.

Coming over! Bringing parents and everything!

Hi, Mr. Williams! Hi, Dr. Williams!

Can we help set up?

I asked Dr. Williams to take paintings off the wall. She's a surgeon, so she has careful hands. We used the hooks to hang my parents' suits.

We also put up the hearts and photo frame.

My living room looked like a suit shop . . . decorated for Valentine's Day.

The doorbell rang at 5:01 p.m. I stopped breathing. Then I remembered my parents would not ring the doorbell.

Everyone was dressed up. Sammy was in a tuxedo!

Aww! Your tux looks awesome, Sammy!

Yeeks! I need to get changed!

I found my blazer. It's like a suit jacket without matching pants.

Um, so I've grown.

Roll up the sleeves. Nobody will know.

Waiting for a party to start is difficult. I had to keep myself busy.

I turned on music.

I reorganized snacks.

I turned all the hooks the same way.

All of a sudden, Sammy ran around the room shouting.

Quack! Quack!

I froze. My parents were home!

Saturday Late Afternoon

Baba looked totally shocked when he saw the party. And even though Ma knew about it, she looked amazed, too.

Surprise!
Happy anniversary!

The perfect FIT!

CUT from the same CLOTH

Happy 'versary!

My parents walked around the suit shop.

The perfect FIT!

Wow!
Look at all this!

CUT from the same CLOTH

Baba meeting Dida and Dadu

Business trip to Seattle with Baby Priya

Dressed up to vote

I felt really proud, like my whole body was full of rainbow emojis. My parents were having fun. I could tell.

I forgot we still had these suits.

Maybe you could donate them. Then other people could wear them to job interviews!

Excellent idea! Thanks for this wonderful party!

TAILOR-made for love

Reeta and Ashok, we have a card for you.

We do, too!

Sammy and I made cards, too.

Sammy

I helped Ma and Baba open the cards.

Happy anniversary, Ashok and Reeta!
We are happy to celebrate you
and help manatees.

The Williams Family
Ron, Jennie, Melissa,
and Harry

Wishing our friends many
happy years ahead. For your
anniversary, we would like to
make a donation to help
manatees.

Layla & Vivek

So proud of my children!
(And grandchildren!)
Let's party for the manatees!

Lots of love,
Dida

Samir

Ma and Baba, happy
Anniversary!
Nobody has parents as
Awesome,
Terrific,
Excellent, and
Especially WEIRD like you!
Sorry, but it's true!

Love,
Priya

Next, Dida served the pretzels. The first tray disappeared fast. So I got another tray, but I felt embarrassed.

I made the wonky pretzels.

<u>DOUGH KNOT</u> judge how they look! They taste great!

That joke was <u>KNOT</u> bad!

The party went by fast. It was 7:12 p.m.
Ma and Baba had to leave soon!

They took a photo with their friends.

Then we took a family photo.

Ma and Baba left for dinner. Everyone else stayed to help clean up.

Melissa's dad helped me send the donation to help manatees.

Success!

After people left, Dida let Sammy and me eat cereal for dinner. Sammy wanted to watch the movie from Fun, Fun Friday again. I didn't mind. I was happy to snuggle and relax.

NEXT UP

Sunday

Dida and I woke up early and made pancakes.
I ate mine with maple syrup. Dida ate hers
with mango pickle.

I feel proud and happy. I love helping the planet, one AWESOME party at a time!

Priya Chakraborty

Aren't my parents cute? They really SUIT each other.

Susan Patel

Happy anniversary, Ashok and Reeta! 😊

Vivek Shenoy

Blessings to you all! 😄

Neda Nasser

Many more joyful years ahead! 😇

Dola Abiola

Hey, P! Could you plan a party for Prince and his puppy friends at the dog park? Please say yes. 😏

Of course I said yes to Dola! So next up . . . puppy party!

DIY YOUR PARTY!
CARDBOARD HEARTS

Collage a heart with words, art, and creative decorations.

WHAT YOU'LL NEED

- Paper and cardboard
- Pencil
- Scissors
- Paint or markers
- Glue
- Any fun supplies you have, like beads, buttons, or stickers

GET STARTED

1. Fold a paper in half. Draw a half-heart shape. Cut along the line.

2. Unfold and trace the heart shape on cardboard.

3. Cut the heart shape out of cardboard.

4. Color your heart with paint or markers.

5. Decorate your heart. Glue decorations or add designs to make it look the way you want. Get creative!

Write your name.

Draw a picture.

Save the manatees!

Write a short message.

Make a collage.

PARTY TIME

Display your cardboard heart—or share it with someone special.

HOW MUCH DO YOU KNOW ABOUT
TOP SECRET ANNIVERSARY?

 1 Would you like it if someone threw you a surprise party at your house? Why or why not?

 2 Priya shares four facts about manatees on page 14. Do some research! Can you come up with two new facts?

3 Priya enjoys hearing Dida's stories. Ask someone you know to share a memory. What did you learn about them?

 4 Priya wears her blazer with the sleeves rolled up because she's outgrown it. Draw an outfit that you've outgrown. How can you keep wearing it—to help save the planet like Priya?

 5 An acrostic is a poem where the first letter of each line spells out a word. On page 65, what word does Priya's poem spell out? Write your own acrostic! First, write a word going down the page in capital letters. Then add a short line that starts with each letter.

ABOUT THE CREATORS

 **Mitali Banerjee Ruths** grew up in Texas and was a LOT like Priya when she was younger. She wanted to start a business, save the planet, and help endangered animals.

Mitali now lives in Canada. She still cares about animals, protecting the environment, and finding ways to be a better earthling. Mitali loves eating plants, moving slow, and feeling peaceful like a manatee.

 Aaliya Jaleel loves illustrating books with bright, bold color palettes and exciting, lovable characters. When she is not drawing, she's planning fun parties that never quite go as planned—but that turn out memorable nonetheless.

Aaliya currently lives in Texas with her husband. She loves exploring and finding hidden treasures when traveling to new places.

The Party Diaries

Read more books!

1

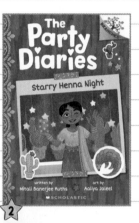

2

4